It's Just Me, Emily

ANNA GROSSNICKLE HINES

Clarion Books
TICKNOR & FIELDS: A HOUGHTON MIFFLIN COMPANY
New York

For just Lassen
just Sarah
and
just Bethany

Clarion Books
Ticknor & Fields, a Houghton Mifflin Company
Text and Illustrations
© 1987 by Anna Grossnickle Hines
Printed in Italy

Library of Congress Cataloging-in-Publication Data
Hines, Anna Grossnickle.
It's just me, Emily.

Summary: Emily pretends to be various creatures
and Mother guesses what they are.
[1. Mothers and daughters—Fiction.   2. Play—
Fiction] I. Title.
PZ7.H572It   1987   [E]   86-34352
ISBN 0-89919-487-7   PA ISBN 0-89919-853-8

NI 10 9 8 7 6 5 4 3

What is that
    under Mother's covers
        down by her feet
            wiggling and twitching
                and tickling her toes?

"Do you suppose," Mother says,
"it might be the cat?

WIGGLE

"Or a weasel perhaps,

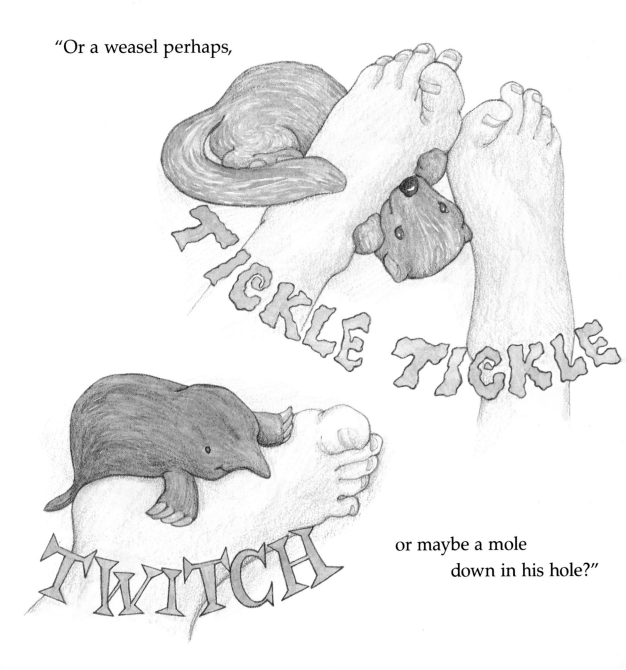

or maybe a mole
down in his hole?"

"No! It's just me...Emily."

From behind the door
comes a terrible roar
a howling and growling
a fierce sort of yowling!

"Oh dear!" Mother cries.
"A lion or tiger must be in there,
or a bear.

"Some horribly fierce and
ferocious beast at least!"

"No! It's just me...Emily."

Under the table there's a thumping and bumping.
It rattles the silver
                    and sets the cups jumping.

"It could be an elephant
or even a rhino…

"or maybe some sort of medium-sized dino!"

"No! It's just me...Emily."

Splish! Splash!
Slip! Slosh!
Swish! Swash!

"Is that a porpoise in the tub,
   or maybe a hippopotamus?
"Or a fat old walrus splashing about
   and pushing all the water out?"

"No! It's just me...Emily."

Zip! Whiz! Zoom! Dash!
It goes by in a streak
in a blur
in a flash!

"Whoa there!" cries Mother.
"Is that a cheetah loose in the house?
A kangaroo from the zoo?

"Or a hurrying
          scurrying
                    giant-sized mouse?"

"No! It's just me...Emily."

From behind the chair comes a happy sound,
a voice softly singing,
"Tra loo tra lay
Oh happy day!"

"Now what could be singing 'Tra loo tra lay'?
Would a bird sing 'Oh happy day'?

Happy Day

"I suppose it might be an elf," Mother says,

Ira Lay

Ira Loo

"or a fairy."

"No, Mama, no. It's just me...Emily."

Everything is so quiet.
Mother can't hear a sound.

No thumping or bumping.
No howls and no yowls.
No giggles or wiggles.

No zipping or dashing.
No splishing and splashing.
Not a sound…not a peep.
"Do you think it could be…? Shhhhhh!

"Yes. It's just Emily."